Presented to:

_____

With love from:

_____

On this date:

_____

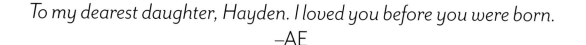

To my dearest daughter, Hayden. I loved you before you were born.
—AE

For Leo and Cameo, I'm So Glad You Were Born.
—KB

ZONDERKIDZ

I'm So Glad You Were Born
Copyright © 2022 by Ainsley Earhardt
Illustrations © 2022 by Zondervan

Requests for information should be addressed to:

Zonderkidz, 3900 Sparks Drive, Grand Rapids, Michigan 49546

Hardcover ISBN 978-0-310-77702-1
Ebook ISBN 978-0-310-77667-3

Library of Congress Cataloging-in-Publication Data

Names: Earhardt, Ainsley, 1976- author. | Barnes, Kim, illustrator.
Title: I'm so glad you were born / by Ainsley Earhardt ; [illustrated by
  Kim Barnes].
Other titles: I am so glad you were born
Description: Grand Rapids : Zonderkidz, 2022. | Audience: Ages 4-8. |
  Summary: Inspired by Scripture, a parent shares their hopes, dreams, and
  joy for their extraordinary child.
Identifiers: LCCN 2022003417 (print) | LCCN 2022003418 (ebook) | ISBN
  9780310777021 (hardcover) | ISBN 9780310776673 (ebook)
Subjects: CYAC: Stories in rhyme. | Parent and child--Fiction. |
  Love--Fiction. | LCGFT: Stories in rhyme. | Picture books.
Classification: LCC PZ8.3.E118 Iam 2022 (print) | LCC PZ8.3.E118 (ebook)
  | DDC [E]--dc23
LC record available at https://lccn.loc.gov/2022003417
LC ebook record available at https://lccn.loc.gov/2022003418

All Scripture quotations, unless otherwise indicated, are taken from The Holy Bible,
New International Version®, NIV®. Copyright © 1973, 1978, 1984, 2011 by Biblica, Inc.® Used by permission.
All rights reserved worldwide.

Illustration: Kim Barnes
Content contributor: Barbara Herndon
Editor: Megan Dobson
Design and art direction: Cindy Davis

Printed in Korea

22 23 24 25 26 27 28 / SAM / 21 20 19 18 17 16 15 14 13 12 11 10 9 8 7 6 5 4 3 2 1

I'm So Glad You Were Born

Celebrating Who You Are

#1 *New York Times* Bestselling Author

Ainsley Earhardt

illustrated by

Kim Barnes

ZONDER**kidz**

It's time to celebrate **WONDERFUL YOU**,
And all the **INCREDIBLE** things you can do.

Let's have a party—a wild celebration!
Cue the thunderous applause and the standing ovation!

Now, come up on stage and accept your award
That spells out exactly how much you're adored.

And I'll bang the drums loudly and blow the brass horn
And shout to the world ...

When you first arrived here, so tiny and new,
The world **JUMPED FOR JOY** at God's big plans for you.

God made you **SPECTACULAR**—one of a kind—
Creatively crafted. Divinely designed.

There's so much to love about little ol' you—
Your kisses and hugs and the kind things you do.

Your smile lights up my heart. Your laughter's a treasure.
And right from the start you've been loved beyond measure.

I'm glad you were born, and I want you to know,

You spread rays of sunshine wherever you go.

I love how you whirl and twirl
through your day,

With dance parties, concerts,
and kitchen ballets.

You're crafty, creative, and smart like a fox,
With your own way of thinking outside of the box.

You bubble with joy when discovering new things—
Like bees give us honey and dragons have wings!

Each day my love for you grows
more and more,
And I'm eager to see what your
life has in store.

God gave you a future that's brighter than bright.
So follow your dreams—let your passions take flight.

The sky is the limit and soon you will see
That you can be anything you want to be.

A builder ...

a baker ...

an electric car maker ...

A mover and shaker ...

a loving caretaker ...

A painter ...

a preacher ...

a history teacher ...

Someone who studies
fantastical creatures.

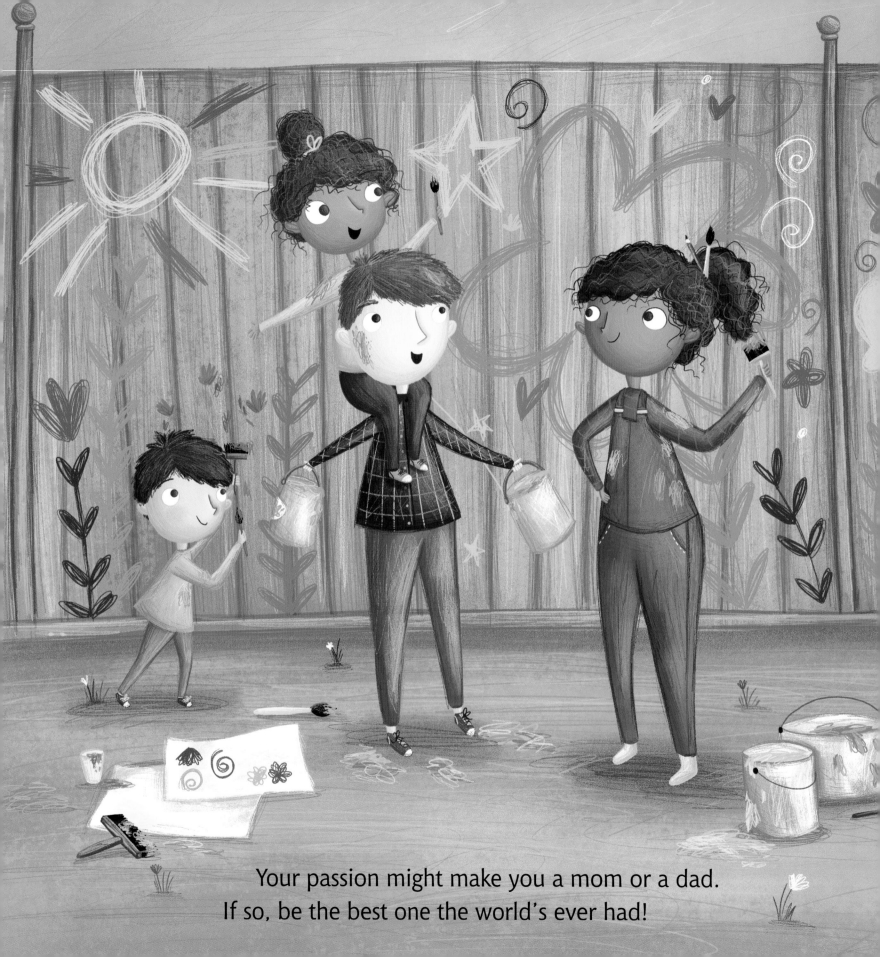

Your passion might make you a mom or a dad.
If so, be the best one the world's ever had!

God's purpose for you is to follow your heart.
Create a **BIG LIFE** that's your own work of art.

And if that life takes you to places afar,
Don't worry, I'll find you wherever you are.

I'll climb any mountain or brave any storm,
To make sure you know …

The world needs your talents and your big heart too,
So lead with compassion in all that you do.

Be honest and true as you show the world you,
And success will come knocking, as if right on cue.

But there may be times when things don't go your way,
When you stumble and fall or you're feeling betrayed.

Don't let mistakes stop you, you're destined to soar.
And soon you'll be stronger than ever before.

On days when you're down
or your heart's feeling torn,

I am always …
ALWAYS …

So glad you were born.

There's no one quite like you on this planet Earth,
So never forget your true value and worth.

You're brilliant of mind, a true one of a kind—
Creatively crafted, divinely designed.

So follow the path that's beneath your two feet
And go out and dazzle the people you meet.

You'll make a big difference wherever you go,
And touch lives of some folks you don't even know.

Keep dreaming your dreams because dreams do come true.
And remember—God has **GREAT BIG PLANS** just for you.

So let's **WHOOP IT UP** at your grand celebration,
And honor the best part of God's great creation.

A party to celebrate you and your dreams,
On **YOUR SPECIAL DAY** and the ones in between.

So bang your drums loudly
and blow your brass horn
And shout to the world ...

I'M SO GLAD I WAS BORN!!!